Glissandra the Glider

Written by
Pamela Galeano

Illustrated by
Daryl Dickson

National Library of Australia Cataloguing -in- Publication data:

Author: Galeano, Pamela Agnes, 1943-
Title: Glissandra the Glider / Pamela Galeano ; illustrator, Daryl Dickson
Publisher: Lower Tully, Qld. : Pamela Galeano, 2008
ISBN   978 0 9804947 0 9 (pbk.)
Notes: 1st ed.
Subjects: Mahogany glider--Queensland--Juvenile fiction.
            Endangered species--Queensland--Juvenile fiction.
Other Authors/Contributors:
            Dickson, Daryl Gay 1954 -
Dewey No: A823.4

Book design & layout by Daryl Dickson Wildcard Art
Illustrations rendered in watercolour on paper
Text of this book in Garamond Premier Pro
Prepress and printing by Bolton Print
Printed in Australia

Author's Dedication

For Tandia and Bronson

Illustrator's Dedication

For all who love our precious wildlife

"You'll have to stay home tonight, Glissy.

You're getting too heavy to glide in my pouch.

You tip my balance,"

said Mother Mahogany.

"I want to come!

Can I glide on your back?

I'll hold on very tight.

And I'll keep very still."

Away they sped through the moist summer air.

Launch – glide – clutch – hide – climb.

Launch – glide – clutch – hide – climb.

How Glissandra loved to glide!

She breathed in the bush smells:

ordinary ones, delicious ones,

snout-wrinkling ones.

She listened to the bush sounds:

ordinary ones, melodious ones, scary ones.

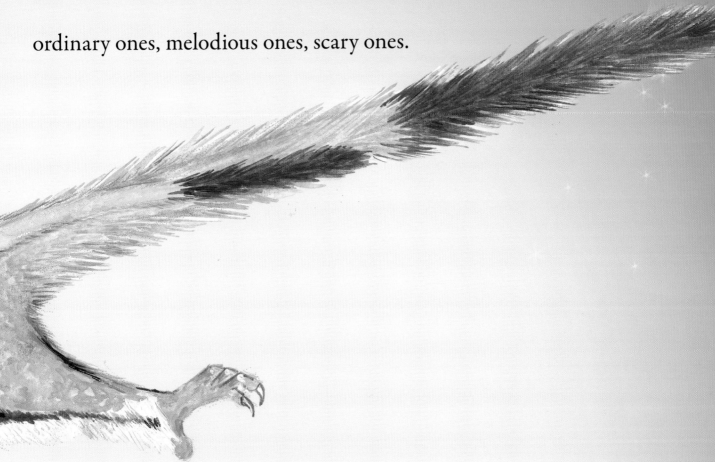

The hoot of an owl made her shudder. But there was a thrill in the

shudder because she was safe with her mum.

Best of all, away from the pouch dark, Glissandra could see!

Her night eyes scanned the paperbarks as they flashed by.

Those curious eyes scanned the forest floor.

They scanned the evening sky.

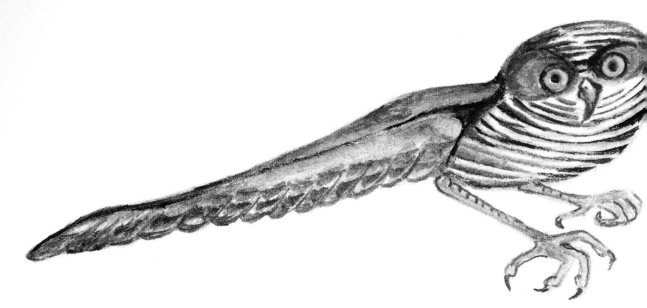

Glissandra was drunk with joy.

Swiftly moving!

Round eyes aglow!

She imagined she was gliding alone.

Her body relaxed and her claws loosened their grip.

Owl attack!

Mother Mahogany swerved.

Glissandra flew straight ahead.

Then she dropped like a rock.

Plop!

She was scrambling in the leaf litter.

Glissandra stared up into the eyes of a hungry Rufous Owl.

With a scream, she dodged a set of monster claws.

She sank her sharp teeth into the owl's leg.

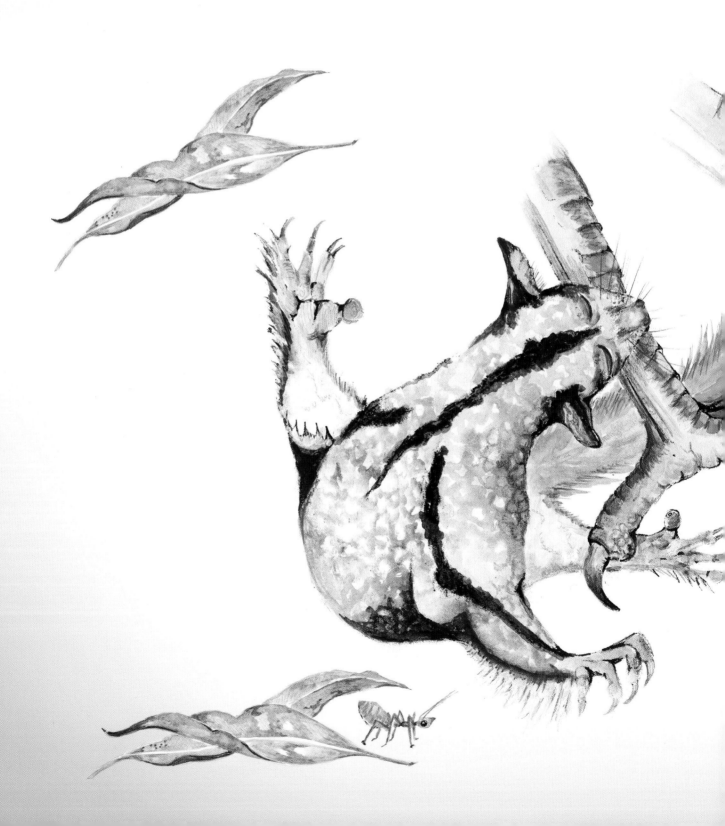

Then she thrust herself backwards into a hole in a rotting log.

Heart pounding, she wriggled further inside, hiding.

She heard a loud swish of wings.

The owl was gone!

Mum would be safely hidden in a tree, but she'd think her

young one was dead.

Glissandra cried, soundlessly.

She had to look after herself.

Turning, she began to creep out the other end of the log.

Her snout recoiled.

Python!

A *full* python is a *safe* python.

She felt snakeskin through her fur as she squeezed silently past.

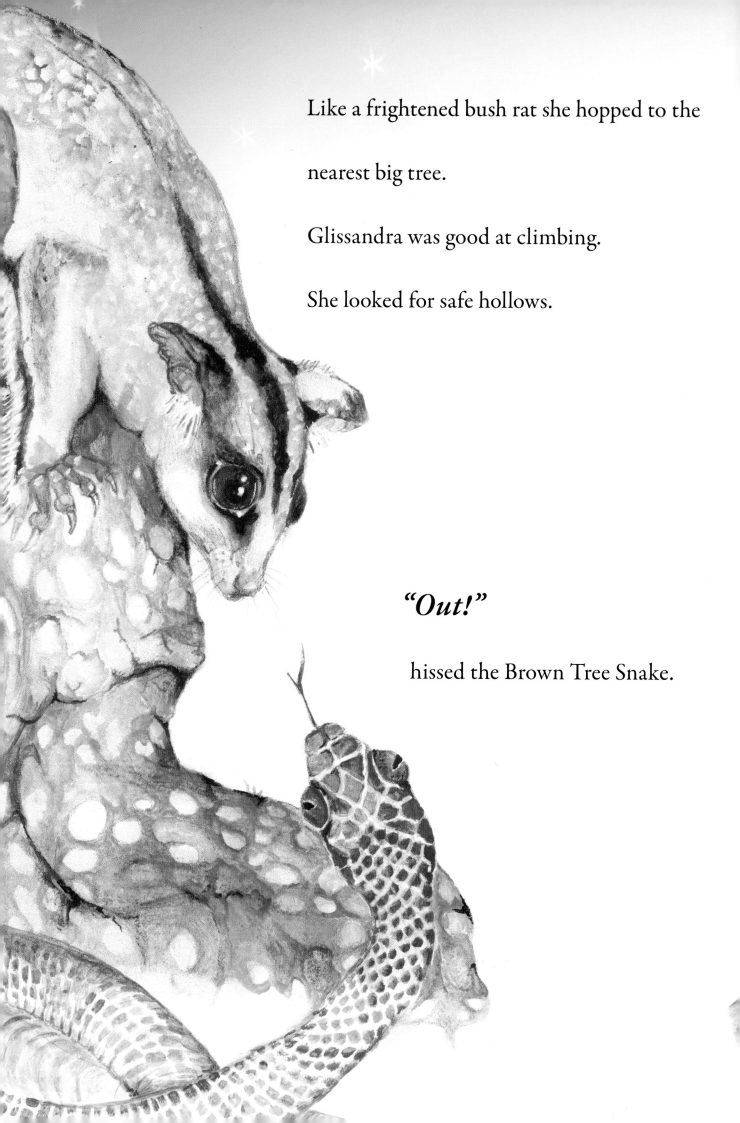

Like a frightened bush rat she hopped to the

nearest big tree.

Glissandra was good at climbing.

She looked for safe hollows.

"Out!"

hissed the Brown Tree Snake.

"Out!"

cackled mother Kookaburra.

"Hello. I'm Sookie," said a young Sugar Glider.

"My family doesn't talk to your family.

But I'm bored and hungry.

Come in."

"Thank you.

I'm Glissandra,

Glissy if you like."

She told her story while they

groomed each other's fur.

"What an adventure," said Sookie.

"Now you'll have to learn to glide. I can't.

But I've been watching a Mahogany Glider licking Ash flowers over there.

That's why I'm so hungry.

He might teach you.

Some of the Ash tree branches touch our tree higher up."

"Thank you, Sookie. Goodbye."

Glissandra carefully followed

the instructions.

Stopping only to lick a few flowers,

she found Mal Mahogany.

"OK, Gliss.

I'll teach you.

But you'll have to concentrate and learn fast."

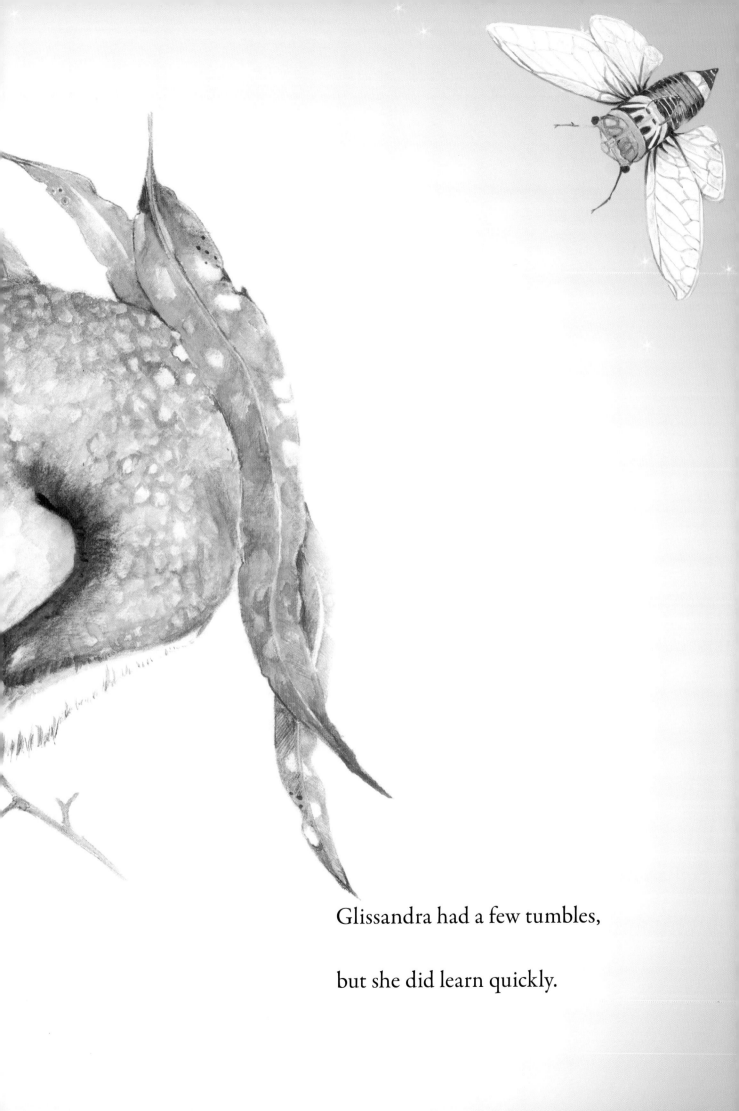

Glissandra had a few tumbles,

but she did learn quickly.

It was Glissandra who first heard the goanna.

She and Mal hid.

While they waited, Glissandra said,

"How will I find my mum again?

We have eight different homes in eight different trees!"

"I have only five homes so far," said Mal.

"My advice is to find your mum's food tree.

It's probably the only other Moreton Bay Ash in the area."

He gave directions.

"Can you glide there by yourself?"

"Yes, thanks Mal.

 I'll see you around."

Glissandra licked a couple more flowers.

She twitched her whiskers and took off on her first big glide.

Launch - glide - clutch - hide - climb.

She was travelling well.

It was time for a rest.

Glissandra remained very still, relaxed, but alert.

Suddenly the tree was alive with fruit bats.

One of them purposely knocked her over.

She held on grimly with her hind claws.

Swinging upright again, she leapt into a nearby Stringy Bark and was gone.

Rain!

Glissandra didn't like wet fur.

She sheltered under a wide branch.

Crunching on a beetle and sniffing the wet earth smells,

she waited.

Then she shook her fur and

flicked her tail.

Off she went again.

Here comes the Moreton Bay Ash.

Glissandra's heart thumped.

She saw three gliders.

She landed on the trunk and hid.

Mum wasn't there?

She heard rustling on the other side of the tree.

"Glissy darling!

How did you escape?"

Glissandra's mother hugged her very tight.

Then she hugged her again.

Rivers of happy tears ran down her fur.

Glissandra was too joyful to speak - just for a little while.

Then, breathing in her mum's very special perfume, she said,

"I can glide!"